HOPE IS HERE!

Written by Cristina Kessler • Illustrated by Marcos Castillo

little bell
CARIBBEAN

Dedications

FROM THE AUTHOR

I dedicate this book to my good friend and domino partner, Mr. Guy H. Benjamin - a true scholar, gentleman, and educator who inspired generations of Virgin Islands students. We all miss you, Benji.

FROM THE ILLUSTRATOR

I would like to dedicate my work to my only love and greatest inspiration, my mother, Oneida del Carmen Guzman. I love you, Mom.

Text copyright © 2013 by Cristina Kessler

Illustrations by Marcos Castillo copyright © Silverwind Production, Inc.

Published by Little Bell Caribbean, an imprint of Editorial Campana

For more information regarding permission, write to:
Little Bell Caribbean
19 W 85th St.
New York, NY 10024
or by e-mail, write to info@campanitabooks.com
Visit us online at www.campanitabooks.com

First edition January 2014

Editor and project director: Mario Picayo
Production: McKinley Matteson
Book design and map illustrations by Yolanda V. Fundora / www.urban-amish.com

"Migration routes of Hope the Whimbrel" map on page 14 by the Center for Conservation Biology at the College of William & Mary and Virginia Commonwealth University (CCB)

Photo Credits:
Cover and back cover photos by **Lisa Yntema**
Page 1: **Lisa Yntema;** Page 3: **Lisa Pirie,** Canadian Wildlife Service; Page 6: Great Pond and fiddler crab by **Lisa Yntema;** Great Pond mangroves by **Fletcher Smith**, Center for Conservation Biology at the College of William & Mary and Virginia Commonwealth University (CCB); Page 7: **Lisa Yntema;** Page 10: **Barry Truitt,** The Nature Conservancy; Page 11: **Bart Paxton**, CCB; Page 12: **Fletcher Smith**, CCB; Page 13: **Lisa Pirie,** Canadian Wildlife Service; Page 14: **Alex Lamoreaux,** CCB; Page 19: Virginia whimbrel habitat by **Fletcher Smith**, CCB; Hope in Virginia by **Barry Truitt**, The Nature Conservancy; Pages 20, 21, 25, 30: **Lisa Yntema;** Page 31: **Fletcher Smith,** CCB; Page 32: **Lisa Yntema.** All photographs used by permission.

Library of Congress Cataloging-in-Publication Data available upon request

ISBN 13: 978-1-934370-43-8

Manufactured in the United States of America

9 8 7 6 5 4 3 2 1

Acknowledgments

FROM THE AUTHOR

I would like to thank Mrs. Cecile Galiber de Jongh, First Lady of the U.S. Virgin Islands, for her dedication to literacy. I would also like to thank field biologist Fletcher Smith for his assistance with fact checking and photos, as well as William and Mary College and Virginia's Nature Conservancy. Also thanks to photographer Lisa Yntema; my first editor, Joe; and publisher Mario Picayo. A special thanks to Alice Krall. Thanks to all the individuals and companies that generously contributed to the publishing of *Hope Is Here!*. May the Virgin Islands blossom with a new generation of bird-watchers!

Great Pond,
St. Croix, U.S. Virgin Islands

Okay, kids, we're here. It is the exact same place I saw Hope two weeks ago. Hope is why we are here. She's a ...

I'm tired!

I'm thirsty!

I'm hungry! And I want to go home. And why are you whispering?

ust drink some water and get comfortable. I'm whispering so we can bird-watch and find Hope if we're lucky.

Where are we again? And what do you mean by 'find Hope'?

We're on Great Pond, sitting quietly while we watch for a bird named Hope.

I'm bored. How long do we have to wait here?

Bored? You won't be bored when I tell you the story of Hope. She can teach us courage, strength, and heart. Let's see who can spot her first.

Please tell us the story, Miss B.

Hope is a whimbrel, a large shorebird, with a story you won't believe.

St. Croix

Miss B. whispered, "Just so you all know, I'll say it again – this is a true story. Hope is the whimbrel we are trying to see today. Every year, from August to May, she lives right here on St. Croix. Our wetlands provide her with what seems like an endless supply of her favorite food – fiddler crabs."

Fiddler crab

GREAT POND, ST. CROIX

Looking left and right she said, "All whimbrels have long thin legs, beaks that curve downward, and long skinny toes. She's got beautiful brown feathers and a light streak down her dark head. You might think Hope looks funny at first, but what she does every year is no joke. You'll know it's Hope for sure by her band – but wait I'm getting ahead of myself."

Whimbrel

Crown (top of head) dark with a distinct light stripe in the middle

Streaked and buffy (brownish) all over

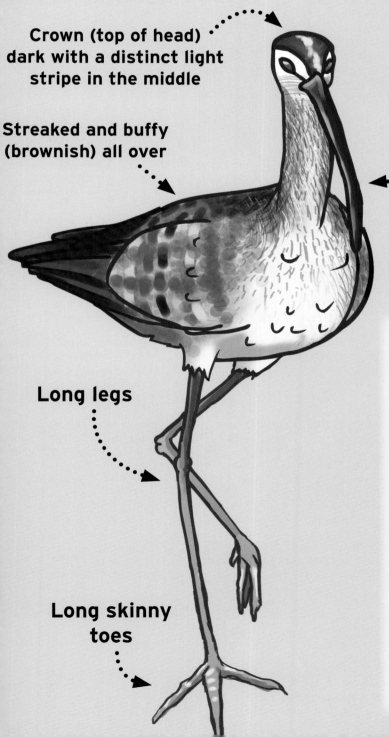

Long, down-curved beak good for digging for crabs in the mud

Long legs

Long skinny toes

Common Name: Whimbrel

Scientific Name: *Numenius phaeopus* (This means "the new moon" in Greek because of the shape of her beak.)

Size: Females are larger than males. Hope is 17 inches long from the tip of her large curved bill to her tail. She has a 32 inch wingspan and weighs 16 to 24 ounces.

Distribution: One of the most wide-ranging shorebirds in the world. Whimbrels breed in the Arctic and migrate to South America, Africa, south Asia, Australia, and the Caribbean.

Diet: Whimbrels love fiddler crabs and other crustaceans, aquatic invertebrates, insects, worms and mollusks. Hope feasts on berries, seeds and leaves on her migration south.

Habitat: Coastal zones and wetlands like Great Pond on St. Croix. They are very territorial. Hope has been spotted within 10 feet of the same spot, protecting her fiddler crab supply, year after year.

Call: A rapidly repeated "tu" sound, like a flute. In flight they make a loud trill and when danger is near, a harsh squawk.

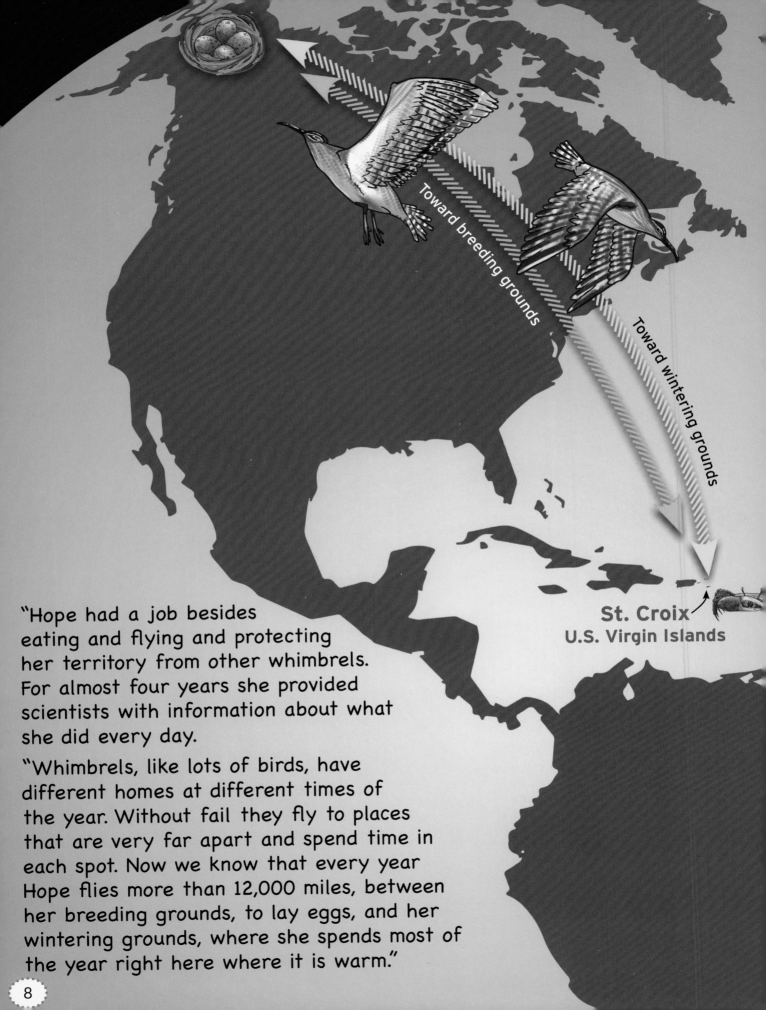

Toward breeding grounds

Toward wintering grounds

St. Croix
U.S. Virgin Islands

"Hope had a job besides eating and flying and protecting her territory from other whimbrels. For almost four years she provided scientists with information about what she did every day.

"Whimbrels, like lots of birds, have different homes at different times of the year. Without fail they fly to places that are very far apart and spend time in each spot. Now we know that every year Hope flies more than 12,000 miles, between her breeding grounds, to lay eggs, and her wintering grounds, where she spends most of the year right here where it is warm."

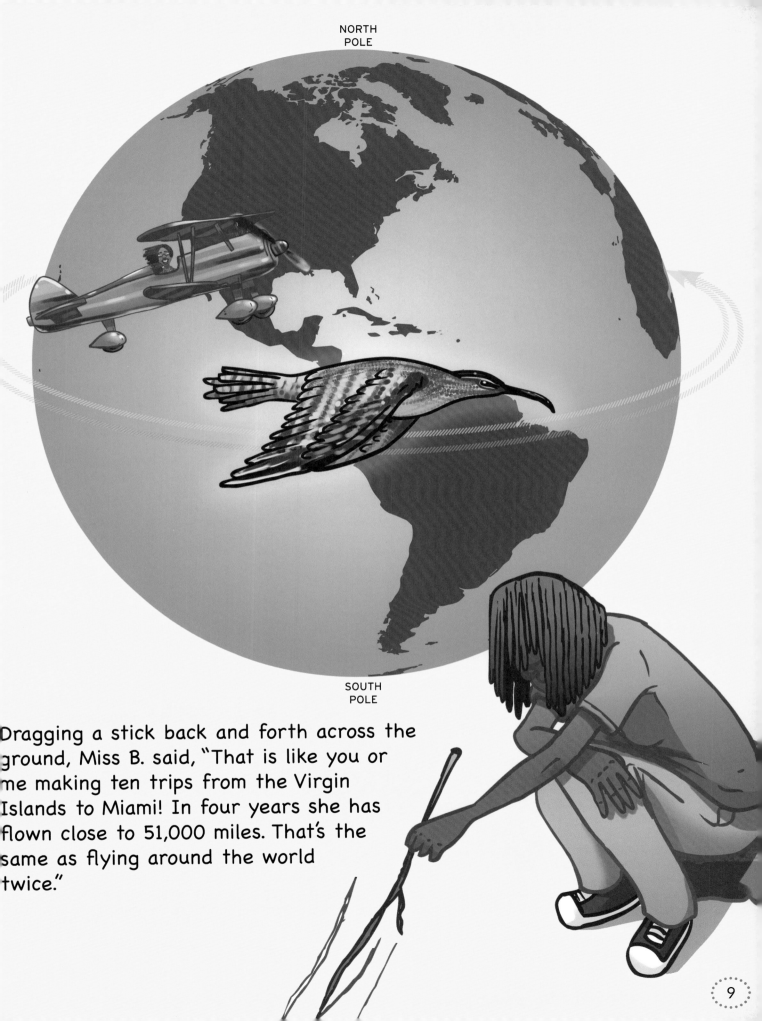

Dragging a stick back and forth across the ground, Miss B. said, "That is like you or me making ten trips from the Virgin Islands to Miami! In four years she has flown close to 51,000 miles. That's the same as flying around the world twice."

Fletcher

Everyone listened quietly while they watched for Hope to appear. Instead, a snowy egret landed.

"In 2009, Hope was caught by a scientist, Fletcher Smith, on Hope Creek in the Virginia wetlands. She was there eating fiddler crabs as fast as she could catch them. Fletcher didn't know where she had come from or where she was going. What he did know was he needed the information to protect the places Hope depends on for food and rest.

"Fletcher knew the best way to gather that information was to place a tiny solar-powered antenna on her back. With this he could follow every mile she flew and every place she landed." Smiling, she said, "I love it - technology and a living bird are the perfect example of science with a heart."

Predators: Adult whimbrels have few natural predators other than foxes or larger raptors. Their biggest threat is humans and the impact we have on their breeding, staging (resting), and wintering sites. Hunters also pose a threat. This is why it's so important for countries to come together to protect all the sites Hope and her fellow whimbrels use on their migration routes.

VIRGINIA — Delmarva Peninsula

The study of whimbrels' flight is being conducted by the Center for Conservation Biology at the College of William and Mary, Virginia Commonwealth University, and the Virginia Chapter of the Nature Conservancy.

Field biologist Fletcher Smith has been closely tracking Hope during four round trips from Virginia to her breeding grounds in the Arctic region of the Mackenzie River Delta in northwestern Canada, to her staging spot in South Hampton Island in the Hudson Bay of Canada, to her wintering spot in the wetlands of Great Pond on St. Croix in the U.S. Virgin Islands.

Now all the kids were watching Miss B. as she drew another line on the ground.

"Fletcher and bird-watchers around the world followed Hope's travels on their computers as her tiny transmitter sent in live reports. I'm sure you will be as surprised as they were by the trips this bird, the size of a small duck, makes."

Mackenzie
River
Delta

Arctic Circle

★INUVIK

Mackenzie River Delta habitat

Tapping the beginning of the long line she had drawn she said, "The first surprise came when she left Virginia. Hope flew directly to the place where she nests, in the Arctic region of northwestern Canada. Imagine – flying over 3,000 miles in six days!"

Breeding: Whimbrels breed in the Arctic and subarctic from Iceland to Canada, to Alaska and Eurasia. They prefer to nest in low-Arctic moorland close to the tree line. They nest either in shallow holes on the ground hidden by low grass or on a mound of moss or grass with water at the base. A nest usually has two to five eggs and both male and female whimbrels incubate the eggs for 22 to 28 days. Both parents also care for the chicks until they fledge (leave the nest) in 35 to 40 days.

Speckled eggs help keep the nest safe and hidden in the grass.

Tapping the other end of the line, Miss B. said, "Here she makes a nest on the ground and lays her eggs. It's cold and wild up there. No one lives nearby like we do to Great Pond. After breeding, Hope starts the journey back to her wintering grounds on St. Croix."

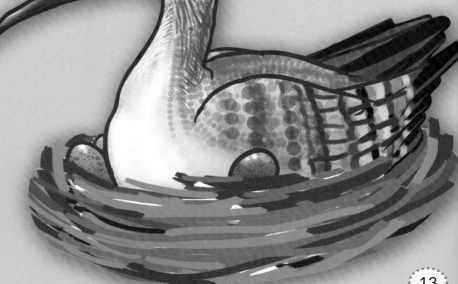

Drawing a new line connected to the first line, she dragged it to the right. "Every year she flies east, usually flying two days without stopping. Her goal is to reach South Hampton Island in Hudson Bay. Her strong wings carry her to almost the exact same spot every time."

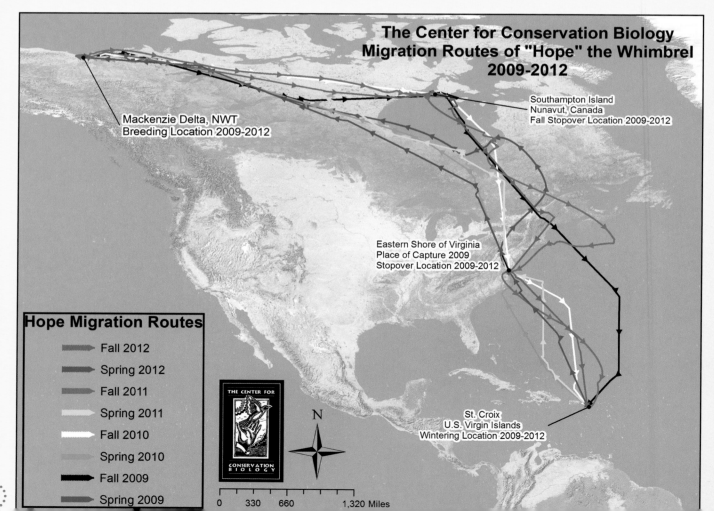

**The Center for Conservation Biology
Migration Routes of "Hope" the Whimbrel
2009-2012**

Mackenzie Delta, NWT
Breeding Location 2009-2012

Southampton Island
Nunavut, Canada
Fall Stopover Location 2009-2012

Eastern Shore of Virginia
Place of Capture 2009
Stopover Location 2009-2012

St. Croix
U.S. Virgin Islands
Wintering Location 2009-2012

Hope Migration Routes

Fall 2012
Spring 2012
Fall 2011
Spring 2011
Fall 2010
Spring 2010
Fall 2009
Spring 2009

THE CENTER FOR
CONSERVATION
BIOLOGY

N

0   330   660   1,320 Miles

Miss B. smiled and said, "She knows she will find the food on the island to make her strong for the next leg of her journey, back here to St. Croix. She eats until she's so full she won't have to stop on her trip. Once for three weeks she gobbled down blueberries, cloudberries, and crowberries, turning her long narrow beak purple."

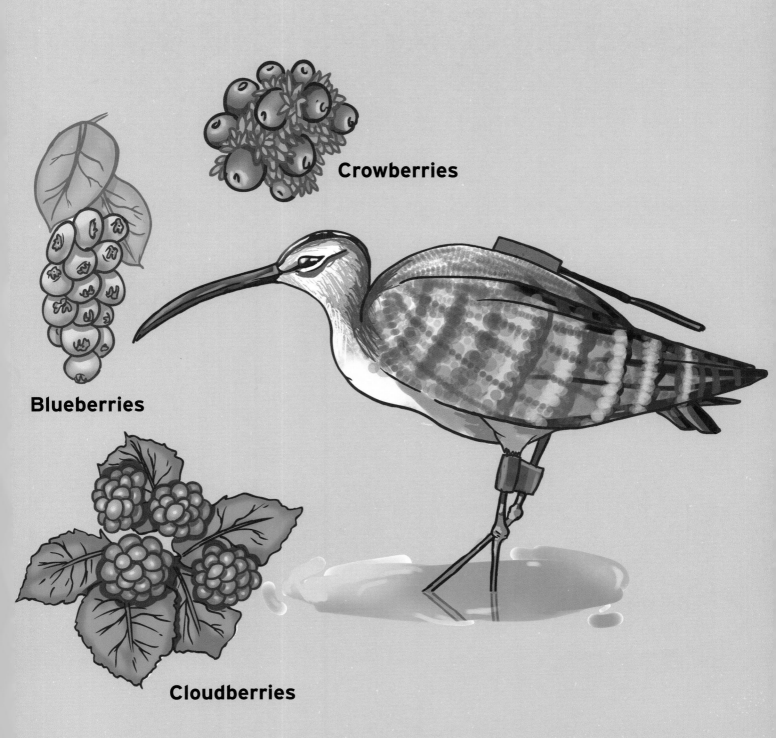

Crowberries

Blueberries

Cloudberries

Leaning forward she said, "You won't believe what happened next. Fat from her berry feast, Hope headed toward the open sea and south. For two days she zipped along at 43 miles per hour until she flew straight into Tropical Storm Gert. Imagine something so small flying right into a storm."

"What happened to her?" asked a nervous Jack.

"Did she make it through the storm?" asked Lubna.

Did she make it through the storm?

What happened to her?

Miss B. patted their hands as she whispered, "For two days she flew into strong headwinds and her speed dropped down to only nine miles per hour, like a car in a traffic jam. But Hope never gave up."

Feeling everyone's tension she said, "Finally she broke through to the storm's other side and zoomed like a pebble from a slingshot, 92 miles per hour. In an hour and a half she flew straight to the nearest land, Cape Cod. There she rested after four days of nonstop flying and fighting a major storm." Deep sighs of relief could be heard.

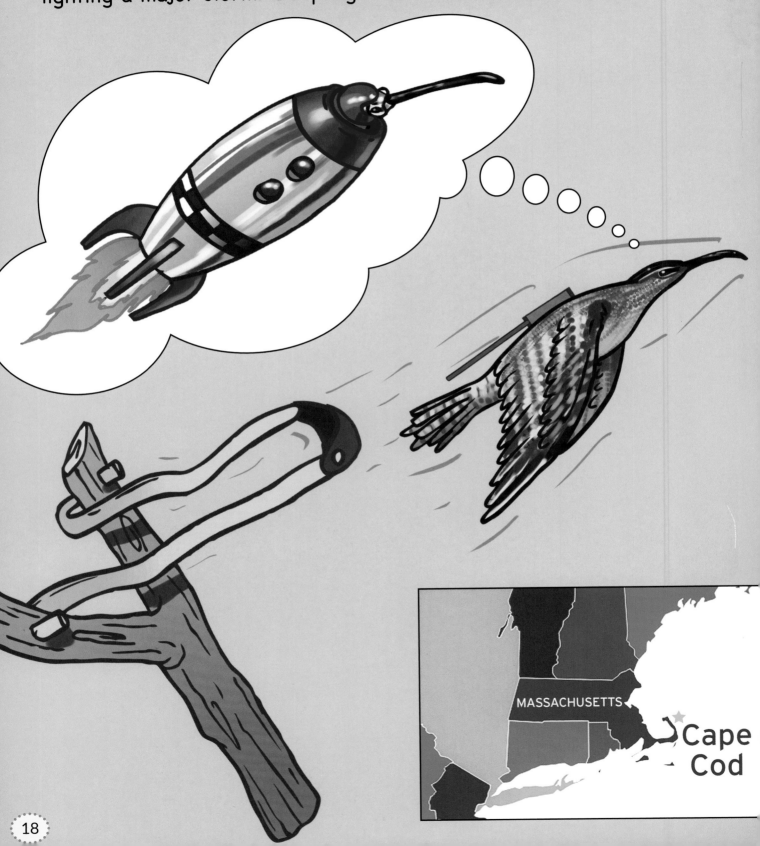

MASSACHUSETTS

Cape Cod

Virginia whimbrel habitat

Cape
Cod

MASSACHUSETTS

VIRGINIA

Delmarva
Peninsula

Hope with other whimbrels in Virginia

Drawing another line down, Miss B. said, "And still her journey wasn't finished. First she flew back to the same place in Virginia where they put the equipment on her. There she rested and ate lots of crabs to give her strength for the last leg of the trip."

Drawing another line that ended with a star, Miss B. whispered, "As if she hadn't already flown across North America, then through a storm at sea, she flew south for two days without stopping. Finally, Hope landed safely on St. Croix." Brianna and Luis silently high-fived each other to celebrate her safe arrival.

★ CHRISTIANSTED

FREDERIKSTED

Great Pond

St. Croix

N

Broken antenna

Pointing across the ground in front of them, Miss B. said, "We'll know Hope when we see her because now she wears a green band attached to her leg. In November 2012, Fletcher came to St. Croix to find Hope. Her antenna no longer worked, and he wanted to catch her to remove it."

"For three days Fletcher sat in a camouflage tent right here, watching Hope and waiting to catch her. When he caught her, Fletcher removed the solar-powered antenna, and then he set her free.

"Hope sounds like Super Bird!" said Luis. "She sure is," whispered Miss B. "Hope has provided more information than any other whimbrel. Through her help, we now know what areas to protect, like right here at Great Pond."

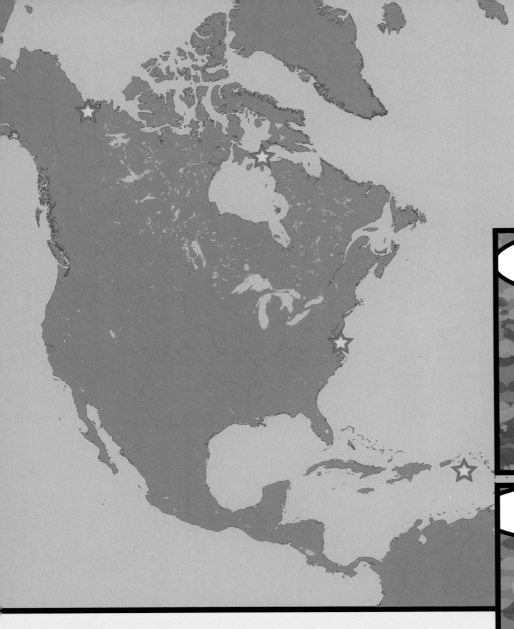

With a twinkle in her eye Miss B. asked, "Can anyone name her other places?" Kareem's hand went up, "The Arctic in Canada." Lubna whispered, "Hudson Bay." And Alice said, "Virginia."

Clapping her hands, Miss B. said, "Excellent! And so my fellow bird-watchers, we all now know the story of Hope."

Afterword

Even without her antenna we are still able to follow Hope thanks to the green leg band she still wears. In March 2013, photographer and naturalist Lisa Yntema and I had the pleasure of seeing her. Lisa had not seen her for over five weeks, so she was very happy when a healthy Hope stepped forward. After snacking on something tasty from the mud, Hope turned and looked at us. The green band on her upper leg told us that it was Hope. Together we said, "Hope is here!"

On August 23, 2013, Lisa saw Hope at a new location on St. Croix, at Southgate Pond. She was with a group of very tired whimbrels. Lisa thought she was there because the water was the perfect depth for feeding. It was surprising because she had never gone anywhere else in St. Croix while wearing her transmitter (proving that we still have a lot to learn). Six days later on August 29th Hope was back in her old stomping grounds at Great Pond. Then, on September 4th, Lisa and a friend saw her there again. It's great to know that Hope is here again.

HOW KIDS CAN HELP THE ENVIRONMENT

1. Join, or help organize, a clean-up day at a beach, park, or wetland.

2. NEVER litter. Always put your trash in the garbage can.

3. Plant a tree, a bush, or flowers – maybe a plant that produces food you can eat!

4. Don't waste water – take shorter showers!

5. Don't waste electricity – shut off lights not being used and other electrical things.

6. Don't waste paper – use both sides and use recycled paper when possible.

7. REDUCE – Buy less stuff.

8. REUSE – Use again whatever you can, like jars, boxes, and bags.

9. RECYCLE – Save things like aluminum cans that can be processed and used again.

10. Spend time in nature and enjoy!

Glossary

BREEDING GROUNDS - Places where animals go to raise their young.

CONSERVATION - The careful preservation and protection of something. Can be of a natural resource, like wetlands, a forest, or a beach. Conservation of a natural resource includes preventing the area from being spoiled by development or pollution.

HABITAT - The place where an organism lives.

MIGRATION - The regular movement of birds and many other creatures from one part of the world to another and then back again. It is one of the wonders of the natural world.

SOLAR POWER - Using the sun as a source of energy.

SPECIES - A specific kind of living organism. A whimbrel is a species of bird.

TRANSMITTER - An instrument that transmits or sends electromagnetic signals to another instrument (or machine) that can receive them. The short antenna that showed where Hope was at all times, including how fast she was flying and for how long, is a transmitter.

WETLANDS - Any area of freshwater or marsh, including flowing water and canals. These rich, usually soggy places provide a habitat for numerous species, help clean our water, control floods, and provide plenty of food for humans. It's important to protect and save wetlands for plants, animals, and people.

WHIMBREL - A species of shorebird known for its long-distance migrations.

WINTERING GROUNDS - Places where many animals spend the winter because of the warmer weather. In most cases the wintering grounds have great food supplies, but not always: humpback whales eat very little while in their wintering grounds in the Caribbean.

May 19, 2009, Hope was caught on the banks of Hope Creek in Virginia. She was outfitted with ransmitter and immediately released.

y was she caught?

pe was briefly captured so she could become an portant part of a study to follow the migration tterns of whimbrels. She was fitted with a tiny solar-wered satellite transmitter that weighed 9.5 grams, d in place by a Teflon strap. Very little information sted on where whimbrels went when they left their eding grounds, how many stops they make, how g a flight could last, or where they stay in winter. e combination of today's amazing technology and ibrant live animal provides information that will p scientists identify and protect the places these ds breed, fly, rest, and winter. Hope is the perfect ample of science with a heart.

cussion topics and activity:

1. What is migration?
2. Do all animals make a migration every year?
3. Do any groups of people migrate? What are nomads?
4. Why do they migrate? ie: following food sources, warmer climate.
5. Hold a pound weight (rock, bag of sand...) and then add something that weighs 9.5 grams. Do you think it was difficult for Hope to carry the weight?
6. What other animals have been tagged to give us information?

at information has Hope provided?

pe has revealed information that left everyone tching her amazed. As the director of the Center Conservation Biology, Bryan Watts says, "Hope s been a real champion." She has recorded close 51,000 miles of flight during her four migrations. cording to Fletcher Smith, "What we learned from pe is that she relies on very, very few places on e Earth to stop, fatten up and move on, whether it's breeding grounds or wintering grounds. If any of ese habitats change, there's real potential for losing ignificant portion of the population." With this ormation they plan to create international programs protect these habitats and save the species.

cussion topics:

1. Why is it important to know where Hope and other animals go?
2. Why do you think Great Pond is Hope's preferred wintering spot?

3. How can you help protect it?
4. What kind of habitat changes do you think could happen?
5. Would you like if someone suddenly came and cut trees near you or built a huge building that took the beach away from you?
6. Great Pond on St. Croix has been designated an "Important Bird Area" by BirdLife International. This listing, and people who care about saving the wetlands, continuously work to protect Hope's home at Great Pond from being developed or polluted. Why is protecting nature important for people, too?

How to become a bird-watcher:

The beauty of bird-watching is that it is free. Patience is very important. Quietly sitting in nature, taking in the sights and sounds, connects us to our natural world. Just in Great Pond alone there are more than 75 species of birds, as well as crabs and other animals to observe. St. Thomas and St. John also have great places to bird-watch. To successfully bird-watch all you need are eyes and birds. Birds are everywhere – outside your window, at the beach, in your backyard. If you want a very close look, binoculars help a lot. To know what you are seeing, use a bird identification book. You never know what you will see, which makes it like going on a treasure hunt every time. There must be a reason there are over 51 million bird-watchers in the U.S. alone!

Class activities:

1. Watch for birds during recess on the playground, or during any outdoor field trips.
2. Organize a bird-watching field trip with someone from the Audubon Society in your area.

Important words for bird-watchers

Binoculars – Glasses that make everything closer and easier to see in detail.

Bird-watcher - A person who studies wild birds in their natural surroundings.

Patience – The ability to sit quietly and wait, while enjoying the sights and sounds of nature.

Shorebird - The North American term for birds that wade in water to find food.

THE AUTHOR

Cristina Kessler is an award-winning author of nine children's books set in Africa, where she lived for 19 years. She's received the Henry Bergh Children's Book Award from the ASPCA for Excellence in Humane Literature for Young Readers; the Africana Honor Book Award, from the African Studies Association, honoring outstanding books about Africa for children and young adults; and has been included many times on The Notable Books for a Global Society list. She always writes about nature or cross-cultural topics.

Cristina has been following Hope for three years now, amazed by her courage and determination. She's an avid bird-watcher who has a personal list of birds from all seven continents. She's even hugged a penguin in Antarctica! In 2001, Cristina and her husband, Joe, moved from the Sahara in Mali to the sea on St. John. She is thrilled to have her first book published set in the Virgin Islands.

To learn more about the author, visit her website: www.cristinakessler.com.

THE ILLUSTRATOR

Marcos Castillo was born in the Dominican Republic, but raised in the Virgin Islands on St. Croix. He graduated from the Columbus College of Art and Design in Ohio with a BFA in illustration. Marcos considers his work to be graphic and stylized yet influenced greatly by the witty voice of street art.

To learn more about the illustrator, visit his website: www.marcosmachina.com.